Padma Shri Pran

Maurice Horn, the editor of World Encyclopedia of Comics, has described cartoonist PRAN as Walt Disney of India.

Entertaining generation after generation, his comics have been constant companion of all the growing youngsters providing fun and amusement through his famous characters like CHACHA CHAUDHARY, SABU, SHRIMATIJI, PINKI, BILLOO, RAMAN etc. More than 600 of his titles are selling well in the market, and numerous comic strips are regularly appearing in various newspapers. His CHACHA CHAUDHARY comics had already been adapted for a TV Serial, and ran continuously for 600 episodes on a premier channel.

Travelling widely over the globe, he delivers lectures at various International Conferences. He has also been honoured with 'People of The Year Award' by Limca Book of Records for popularizing comics. His comic book 'United We Stand' was released in 1983 by the then Prime Minister Mrs. Indira Gandhi, and is still very popular among children.

Publisher

I'M NOT INTERESTED IN WATCHING ANY PLAY. GO AWAY !

DHAMAKA SINGH ! THIS MAGIC WAND HAS IMMENSE POWERS.

GET LOST ! IT'S MERELY A WOODEN STICK.

NOW YOU'RE INSULTING ME. I CAN'T TOLERATE IT.

ABRA !! KAA ! DA-BRAAA !! BECOME A DONKEY.

HEEE !! HOO !!

PLEASE EXCUSE MY BOSS !
LANGOTI IT'S HIS PUNISHMENT.

MAGICIAN POPLI ! I BET! YOU CAN'T CONVERT CHACHA CHAUDHARY AND SABU INTO ANIMALS.

I CAN CHANGE THEM INTO A MONKEY.

CHACHA JI ! WHERE ARE WE GOING?
SABU ! REMEMBER WE SAVED SETH HARIRAM FROM BEING LOOTED.

HE HAS INVITED US FOR DINNER.

SALUTE TO THE MAGICIAN POPLI PASHA.
WHERE'S HE ?
IN FRONT OF YOU.
TO ME YOU SEEM LIKE A JOKER.
IT'S MY INSULT.
AAKRAA !! DABARAA !! FUNKI !! CHACHA BEC....

OHHH !!!
SWISHHH!!!

MY WAND IN YOUR HANDS.
IT'S CALLED MAGIC !

AKRAA !! DABRAA ! FUNKI !! PASHA BECOME MONKEY.

KHOO !! KHO!!
HA ! HA !!

NOW YOU HAD IT.

POPLI ! STAY AWAY FROM MUNICIPAL DEPARTMENT. THEY CATCH STRAY MONKEY.
RUN !!

OH! WHAT'S THIS ?
CHACHA JI MADE ME A MONKEY.

KHO !! KHO !!

DHAMAKA SINGH ! I'M SORRY.

YOU'LL BE PUNISHED.

DHENCHU!!
TIT FOR TAT !!

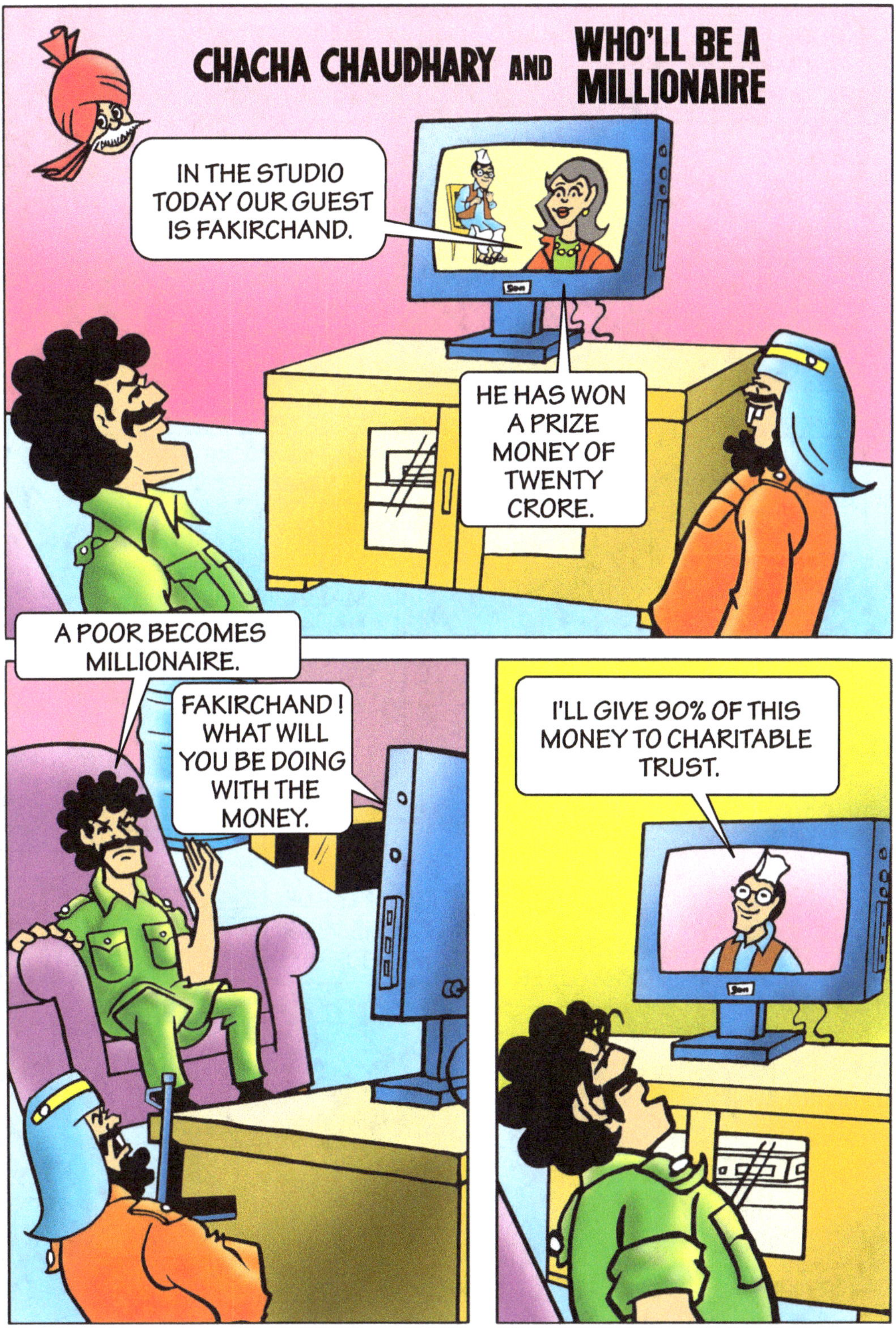

CHACHA CHAUDHARY AND WHO'LL BE A MILLIONAIRE

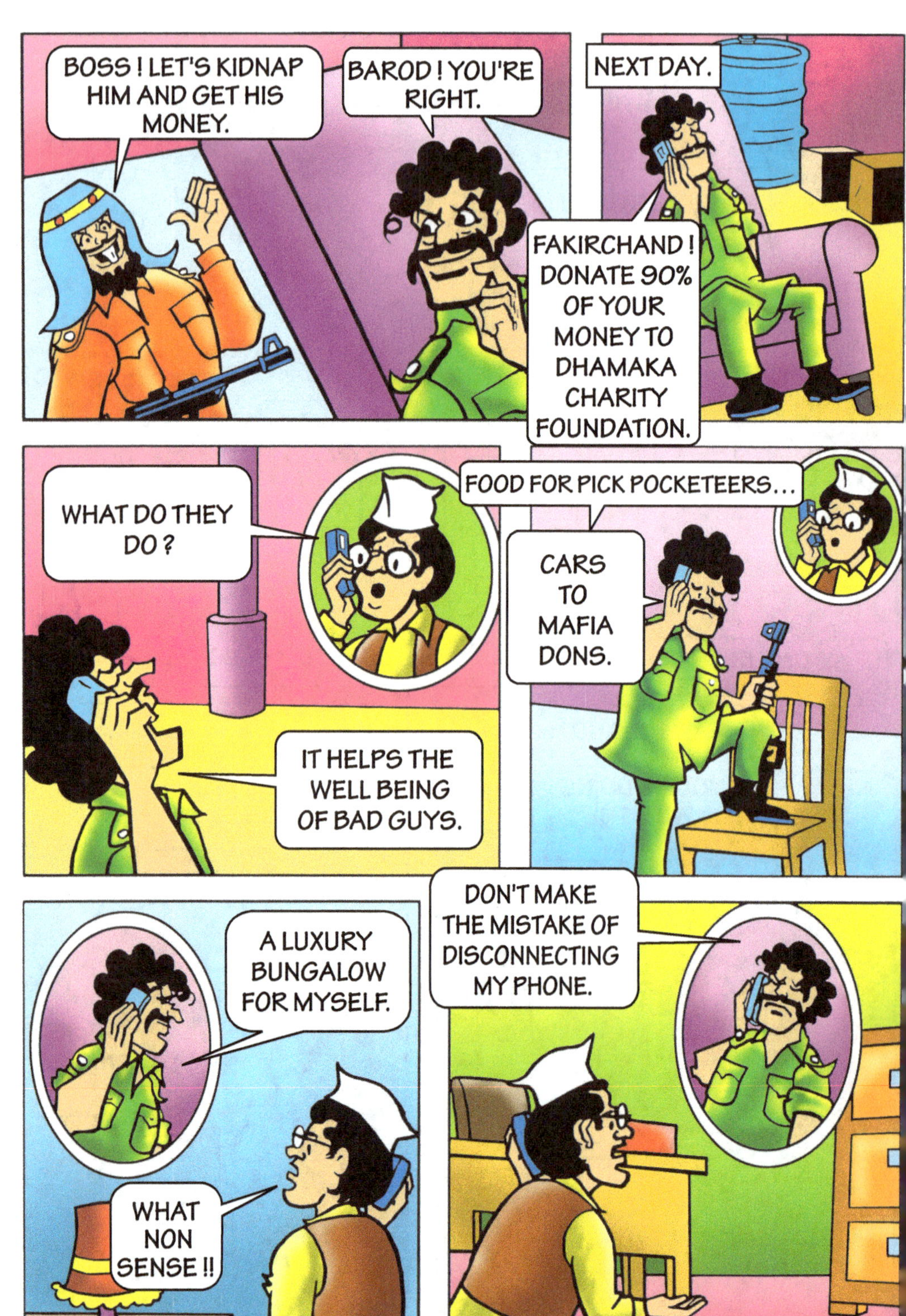

BOSS ! LET'S KIDNAP HIM AND GET HIS MONEY.
BAROD ! YOU'RE RIGHT.
NEXT DAY.
FAKIRCHAND ! DONATE 90% OF YOUR MONEY TO DHAMAKA CHARITY FOUNDATION.
WHAT DO THEY DO ?
FOOD FOR PICK POCKETEERS...
CARS TO MAFIA DONS.
IT HELPS THE WELL BEING OF BAD GUYS.
A LUXURY BUNGALOW FOR MYSELF.
DON'T MAKE THE MISTAKE OF DISCONNECTING MY PHONE.
WHAT NON SENSE !!

NOW! DO AS I SAY.

I'LL COME IN THE EVENING TO TAKE ALL YOUR MONEY.

CHACHA JI! HELP ME. DHAMAKA SINGH IS COMING TO TAKE AWAY MY MONEY.

PLEASE HELP ME.

DON'T WORRY. LET ME SEE.

BOSS! YOUR ORDER.

LET'S GO! BAROD.

I'LL BE A MILLIONAIRE.

ZOOM !!

FAKIRCHAND'S HOUSE IS OPEN.

GOOD ! ELSE I WOULD HAVE BLASTED IT.

FAKIRCHAND ! WE ARE HERE TO TAKE THE REWARD.

NO ONE IS AT HOME ?
THEY HAVE RUN AWAY FROM YOU.

HA ! HA ! EVERYONE IS SCARED OF ME.

HE MUST HAVE KEPT IN BEDROOM.

OH !! TWO LOCKERS ? SMALL AND BIG !!
DUMBO ! TEN PERCENT PRIZE MONEY IN ONE AND REST IN BIGGER ONE.

BOSS ! I'M YOUR CONFIDANT. I'LL TAKE SMALLER ONE.

OK ! DONE.

AHA ! I'LL BE RICH.

OHH !!

BIG BOSS! BIG LOCKER.

!?!

GET LOST!
SWISHHHH!!

SABU! HE WANTS A PRIZE.
I'LL GIVE HIM.

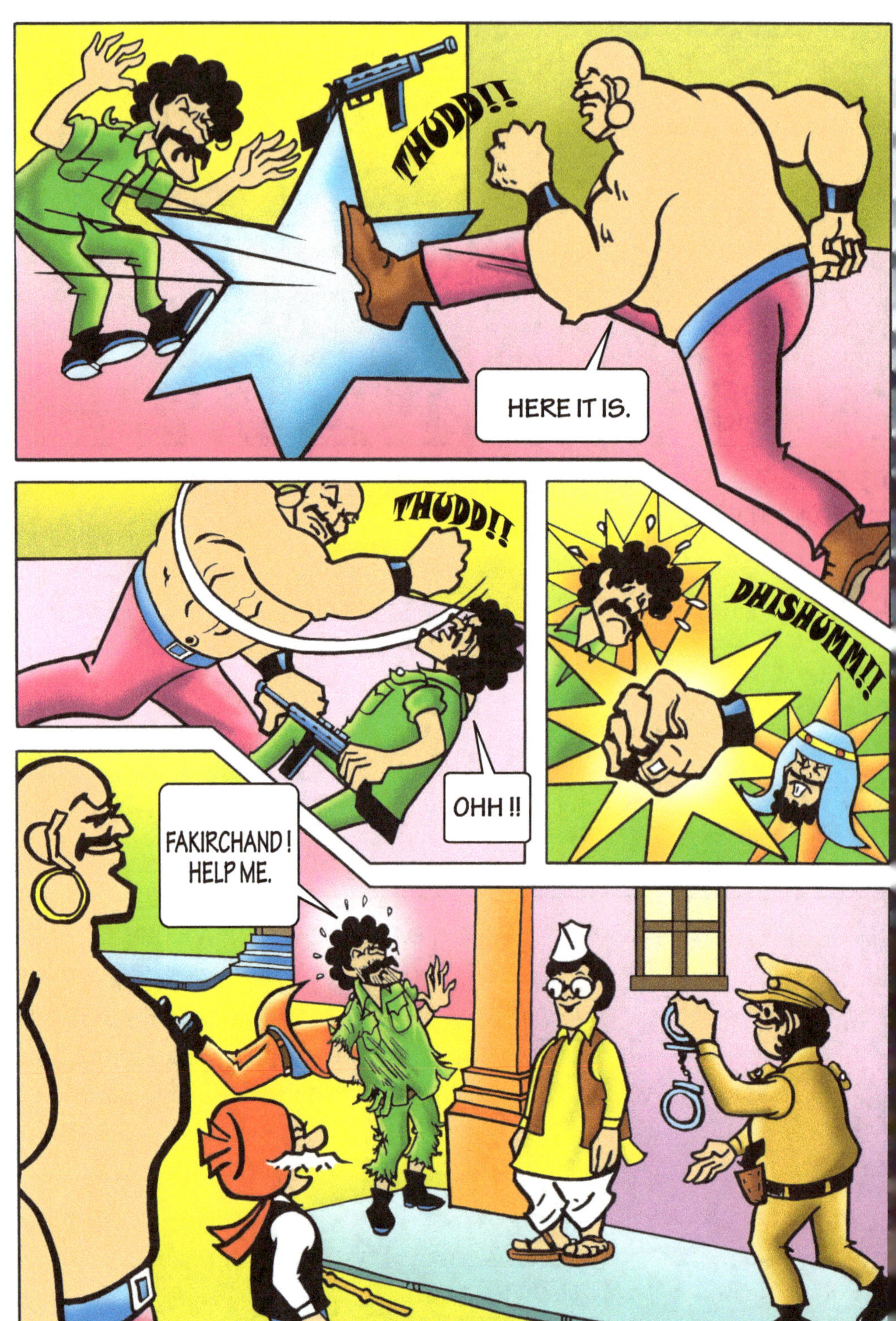

THUDD!!
HERE IT IS.
THUDD!!
DHISHUMM!!
OHH !!
FAKIRCHAND ! HELP ME.

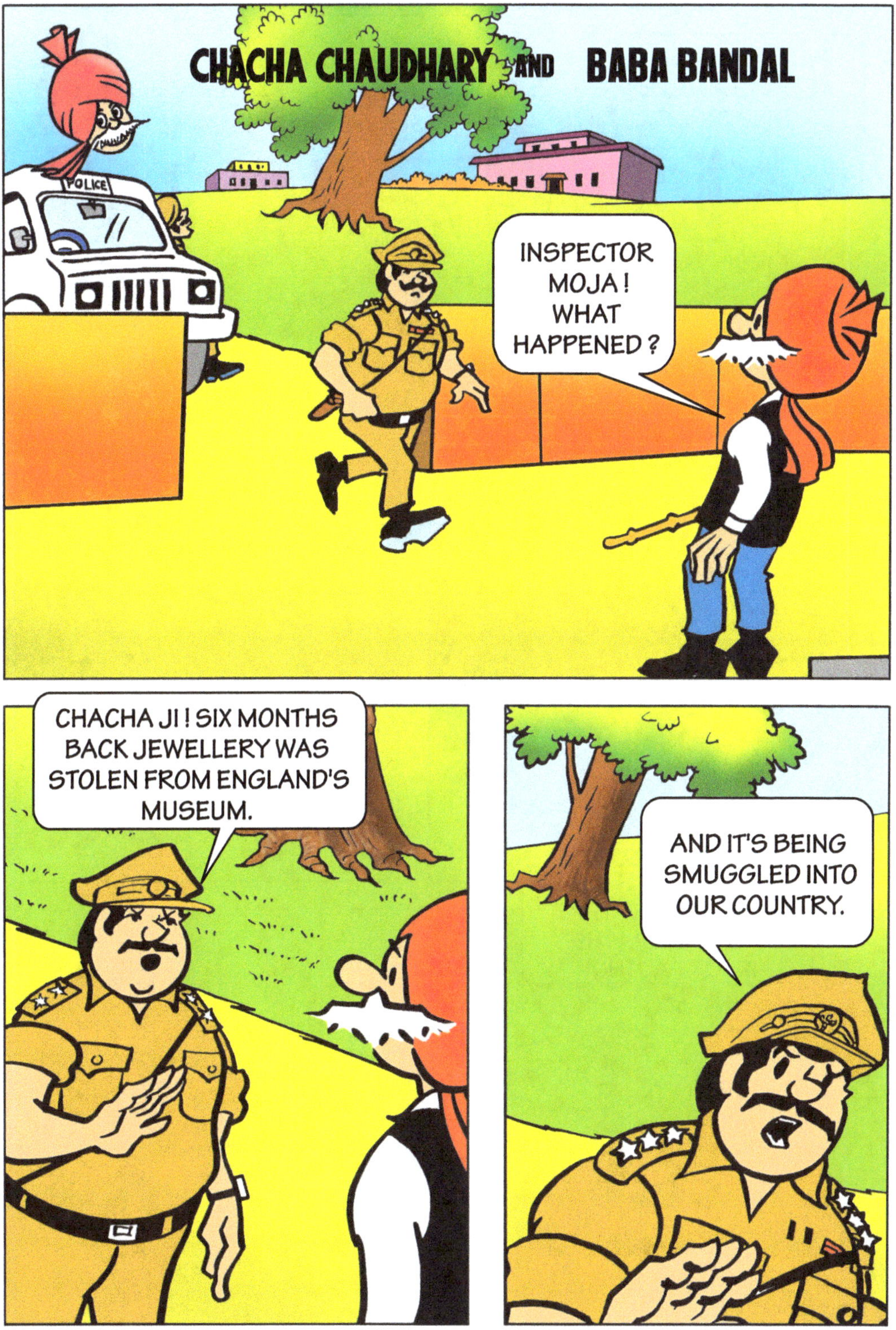

CHACHA CHAUDHARY AND BABA BANDAL

WE HAVE BEEN KEEPING AN EYE ON THE AIRPORT.

EACH PASSENGER IS BEING THOROUGHLY SEARCHED.

BUT WE COULDN'T TRACE THE CULPRIT.

ARRANGE THE LIST OF PASSENGERS WHO HAVE BEEN FREQUENTLY GOING TO ENGLAND.

COME WITH ME. WE CAN GET THAT LIST FROM THE AIRPORT AUTHORITY.
© PRAN'S FEATURES LLP

POLICE
ZOOM!!!

16

AIRPORT
WE WOULD LIKE TO CHECK THE RECORDS OF PASSENGERS GOING TO ENGLAND.
SURE!

LET'S GO TO RECORD ROOM.

OPERATOR! TAKE OUT THE LIST OF ALL PASSENGERS GOING TO ENGLAND.
YES, SIR!

BABA BUNDAL IS FREQUENTLY GOING TO ENGLAND.
HE'S COMING FROM TODAY'S FLIGHT ALSO.

I WANT TO CHECK HIS PROFILE.

HE'S AN INTERESTING CHARACTER.
HE USED TO PERFORM MAGIC SHOWS EARLIER.
I'M CURIOUS TO MEET HIM.

AIRPORT CHECKING COUNTER.
HELLO !! BABA JI !
BLESS YOU !!

WAIT ! WE HAVE TO CHECK YOU.
GREEN CHANNEL
I SPREAD INDIAN CULTURE AND TEACH YOGA IN ENGLAND.
GREEN CHANNEL
DO I LOOK LIKE A THIEF ?
PEOPLE RESPECT ME IN ABROAD AND INSULT HERE.

SABU ! WHY DON'T YOU GIVE A THUMP ON HIS BACK.

EL
NO !!

I DON'T REQUIRE IT.

NO IF AND BUT.

COME HERE !!

20

THUMP !!
THUMP !!
MOJA ! MUSEUM'S JEWELLERY.
CHACHA JI ! HOW DID YOU KNOW IT WAS HIDDEN INSIDE HIS STOMACH.

FROM HIS PROFILE.

HE WOULD PERFORM A MAGIC TRICK...

WHERE HE WOULD TAKE THE WHOLE SWORD INSIDE HIS STOMACH.
I GOT A BIT SUSPICIOUS.*
* CHACHA CHAUDHARY'S BRAIN WORKS FASTER THAN A COMPUTER.
NOW YOU CAN SHOW YOUR MAGIC INSIDE THE JAIL.
Prisoners will be well entertained
POLICE

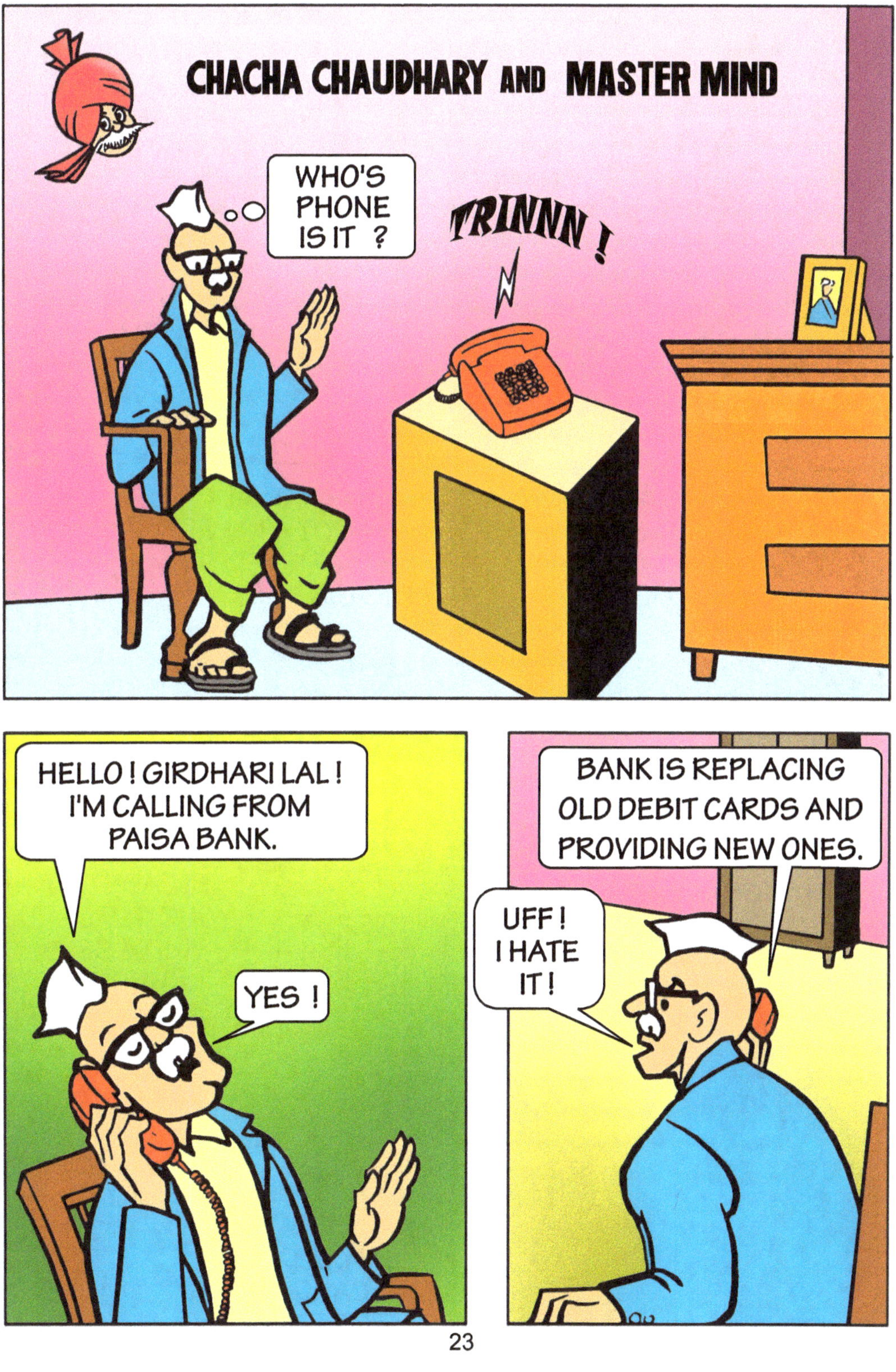

CHACHA CHAUDHARY AND MASTER MIND

I WILL HAVE TO STAND IN LONG QUEUES TO GET IT CHANGED.

NO NEED TO WORRY ! OUR BANK PERSON WILL COME AND GIVE YOU A NEW CARD.
GOOD!

EVENING.
DING ! DONG !!
GIRDHARI LAL ! I'VE GOT A NEW DEBIT CARD FROM PAISA BANK.
COME INSIDE !

WHAT'S THE NEED TO GET IT REPLACED ?
IT'S FOR YOUR OWN SECURITY.
PLEASE GET YOUR OLD CARD AND A SELF CHEQUE.
I'LL GET MY OLD CARD.

HERE IT IS! ANY THING ELSE?
PIN NUMBER OF OLD CARD.

XXXX.
SIGN HERE AND TAKE THIS NEW CARD.

GOOD SERVICE! NO NEED TO GO TO THE BANK.
NEW CARD WILL START WITHIN 15 DAYS.

GO TO ATM AFTER 15 DAYS
OK!

AFTER 15 DAYS.
LET ME TAKE OUT SOME MONEY FOR DAILY EXPENSES.

ATM
MULTI CURRENCY
CARD NOT ACCEPTED
OHH! CARD ISN'T WORKING.

UFF ! I'VE TRIED LOTS OF TIMES.
IT SEEMS LIKE BANK HASN'T ACTIVATED MY CARD.
BANK IS SO FAR.
ATM
MULTI CURRENCY
PLEASE DISPOSE OF ATM RECEIPTS HERE
बैंक

YOU DON'T PITY ON US.
IT'S MY NEW CARD. NOT WORKING.
THIS CARD HASN'T BEEN ISSUED BY US.

CASH
THERE MUST BE Rs 5000 IN MY ACCOUNT.

ALL YOUR MONEY HAS BEEN WITHDRAWAL.
!!!??

I'VE BEEN CHEATED.
ONLY ONE PERSON CAN SOLVE IT.

HE'S CHACHA CHAUDHARY.
YES ! WHOSE BRAIN WORKS FASTER THAN A COMPUTER.
POLICE

POLICE
POLICE TAKE THEIR SALARY FOR FREE. ALL WORK IS DONE BY YOU.
RELAX ! BINI. I DO SOCIAL WORK.

I'VE BEEN CHEATED BY SOMEONE.

HE HAS TAKEN ADVANTAGE OF YOUR OLD AGE.

DON'T WORRY ! WE'LL SOON CATCH HIM.
NOW I'M SATISFIED.

GO HOME AND RELAX.

CHACHA JI ! FROM WHERE DO WE START INVESTIGATING.

IT'S A CYBER CRIME. WILL TAKE THE HELP FROM CYBER CELL.

BOOKS
POLICE
POLICE
SWISHHHHH!!

28

BUREAU CHIEF! I REQUIRE YOUR HELP.
WHAT CAN I DO?
THE MAFIA IS TARGETING SENIOR CITIZENS' BANK ACCOUNT.

THEY FIRST CHECK COMPLETE DETAILS OF THEIR TARGET.
AND SIPHON OFF ALL THE AMOUNT FROM THEIR BANK ACCOUNT.
HERE'S RUKMANI DEVI'S ACCOUNT. WHO SPENDS SMALL AMOUNT EVERY MONTH.
NEED TO KEEP AN EYE ON SUCH ACCOUNTS.

A HUGE AMOUNT FROM HER ACCOUNT HAS BEEN TRANSFERRED TO ...

NEARLY TEN DIFFERENT ACCOUNTS.

FUND IS BEING TRANSFERRED THROUGH MOBILE BANKING.
CHECK ALL THE PROFILES INTO WHICH MONEY HAS BEEN TRANSFERRED.

ALSO CHECK THEIR CALL DETAILS.

CONNECT EVERYONE'S MOBILE TO THE CONTROL ROOM.
CHACHA JI ! NOW YOU CAN HEAR THEIR CONVERSATION.
TRINN !!
MASTER ! TRICK IS WORKING.
MASTER ! THANK YOU. WE'RE ROLLING IN MONEY.
MASTER ! IT'S UNBELIEVABLE.
MASTER ! IT'S A MIRACLE.
MASTER ! YOU ARE GENIUS.

THEY ARE CALLING ONE PERSON THEIR MASTER.
YES ! HE'S THE BRAIN BEHIND THIS.

TAP THE LOCATION OF THE MASTER MIND.

31

THE CALL WAS FROM GOA !
THE SPIDER IS MAKING HIS WEB FROM GOA.

SABU ! LET'S VISIT GOA.

SWISHHH!

WE ARE MOVING TOWARDS THE MOBILE LOCATION.
POLICE
POLICE

WE ARE ENTERING IN GOA.
WE'RE VERY CLOSE.
MASTER! HOW'S THE FENNY.

CHAUDHARY! YOU ??

LOOTING SENIOR CITIZEN'S HARD EARNED MONEY.

YOU'VE MADE A BIG MISTAKE...

BY COMING OVER HERE.

WHAM !

SURRENDER YOURSELF !!
NO ! NEVER !!

NO ONE CAN CATCH ME.
HE'S ESCAPING.

JUMPING LIKE A FROG, LET ME CRUSH HIM.
SORRY!
NEED TO RECOVER ALL THE MONEY LOOTED BY HIM.
HE'LL CONFESS IN THE REMAND ROOM.
POLIC

CHACHA CHAUDHARY AND DOUBLE ROLL

THANKS !

IT'S OUR DUTY.

OHH ! WHO'S BEEN INJURED ?

MUST HAVE MET WITH AN ACCIDENT.

NOW YOU WILL BE HIT.
HAND OVER THAT BAG TO US OR ELSE !!

I'VE TO PAY SALARY.
SAVE YOUR OWN LIFE.

SWISHHH !
CATCH THE THIEVES.

INSPECTOR ! I'VE BEEN LOOTED BY A RED TURBAN THIEF.

CHACHA CHAUDHARY WEARS A RED TURBAN.
HAWALDAR ! THAT'S IMPOSSIBLE.

NEXT DAY.
TODAY WE HAVE TO LOOT A BANK.
YES ! BOSS!

BANG!!
CASH BANK

HAND OVER THE STRONG ROOM KEYS.
BANG!!
CHACHA CHAUDHARY !!
MANAGER

COLLECT ALL WHAT'S THERE.

BREAKING NEWS !!
CITY IS BEING LOOTED BY NONE OTHER THAN ...

CHACHA CHAUDHARY !!

IS THIS A JOKE ?
SOMEONE IS USING ME.

INSPECTOR MOZA ! WHAT'S THIS NEWS ABOUT ME ON TV CHANNELS.
CHACHA JI ! ARREST WARRANT HAVE BEEN ISSUED FOR YOU.

YOU ARE UNDER ARREST.
CHACHA CHAUDHARY, A THIEF.

IT'S A CONSPIRACY.

I'M BOUND BY MY DUTY.

DON'T FORCE ME TO GO AGAINST THE LAW.

RELAX! LET'S SOLVE THIS CASE.

SWISSHH!
POLICE

HELLO! CONTROL ROOM.

CHACHA CHAUDHARY HAS BEEN ARRESTED.
POLICE

WHO'S BEEN CAUGHT?

EVERYONE REACH THE LOCATION.
POLICE

TAKE ME THERE. ALL WILL BE CLEAR.
50%
Books
POLICE

HE'S EXACTLY LIKE YOU.

WE'LL KNOW THE REAL ONE IN A MINUTE.

STORES
BANK
SWISHHH!!

HE'S A DUPLICATE.

EVEN MOUSTACHES.
SWISHH!!

42

WHEN SABU GETS ANGRY A VOLCANO ERUPTS SOMEWHERE.

NOW YOUR TURN.

WAIT !

WHERE ARE YOU HIDING THE LOOT ?
COME WITH ME.

SWISHHH !
POLICE

MOJA ! CONFISCATE EVERYTHING.
THANKS ! CHACHA CHAUDHARY.

FESTIVALS OF INDIA

DIWALI
The Festival of Lights

DURGA PUJA
THE FESTIVAL OF GODDESS DURGA

GANESH CHATURTHI
THE ARRIVAL OF LORD GANESHA

CHRISTMAS
THE DAY OF JESUS CHRIST

DUSSEHRA
The Victory Of Good Over Evil

KRISHNA JANMASHTAMI
LORD KRISHNA'S BIRTHDAY

ONAM
THE HARVEST FESTIVAL OF KERALA

RAKSHABANDHAN
THE PIOUS BOND OF BROTHER AND SISTER

PONGAL
THE HARVEST FESTIVAL OF TAMILNADU

HOLI
The Festival of Colours

BIOGRAPHIES

MAHATMA GANDHI
THE FATHER OF OUR NATION

MOTHER TERESA
THE SYMBOL OF KINDNESS AND LOVE

CHANAKYA
THE PIONEER ECONOMIST OF INDIA

GAUTAM BUDDHA
THE FOUNDER OF BUDDHISM

RABINDRA NATH
THE RENOWNED POET AND SOCIAL REFORMER

CHATRAPATI SHIVAJI
THE GREAT INDIAN WARRIOR

INDIA'S HOPE
NARENDRA MODI

APJ ABDUL KALAM
THE MISSILE MAN OF INDIA

SUBHASH CHANDRA BOSE
THE REVOLUTIONARY LEADER OF INDIA

S. RADHAKRISHNAN
THE GREAT INDIAN PHILOSOPHER

CHILDREN LITERATURE

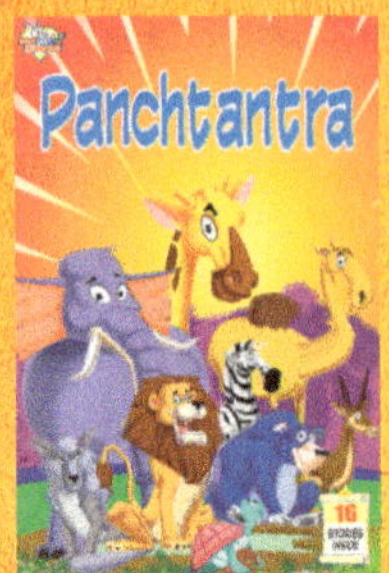

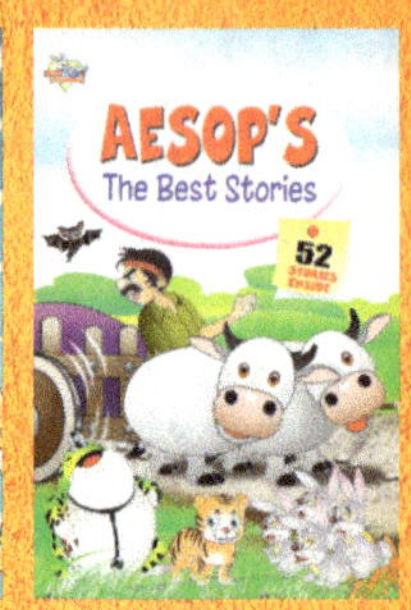

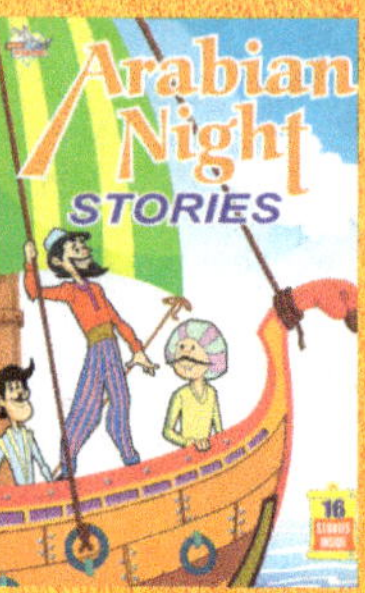

COLOURING & ACTIVITY BOOKS

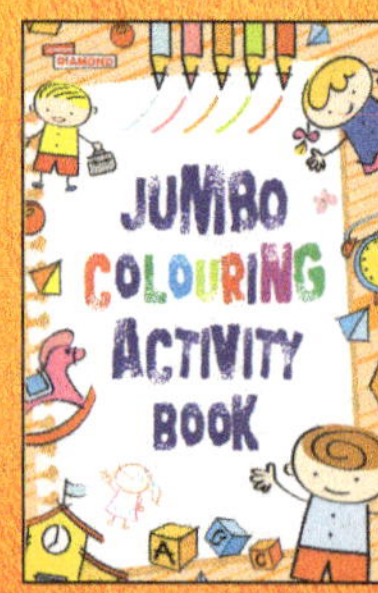

X-30 Okhla Industrial Area, Phase-II, New Delhi-110020
Ph: 011-40712200 e-mail: sales@dpb.in website: www.diamondbook.in

The Largest selling comics in India
Cartoonist Pran's
Billoo, Pinki

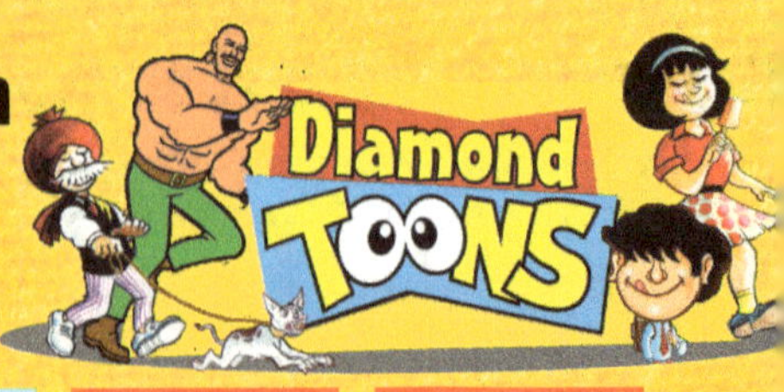

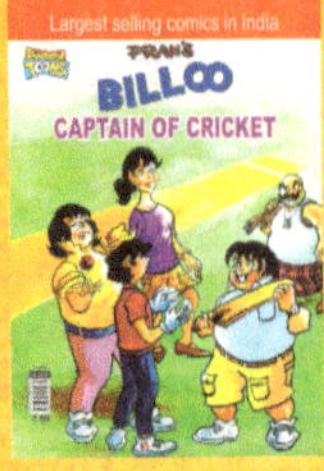

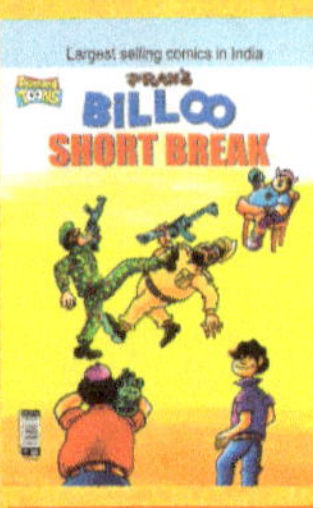

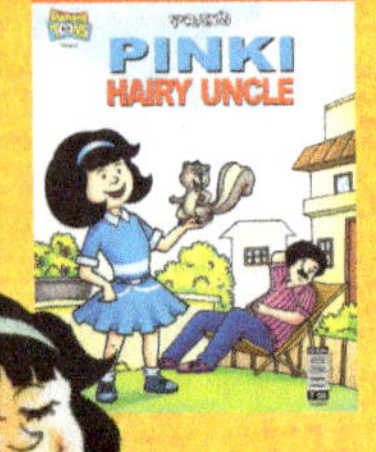

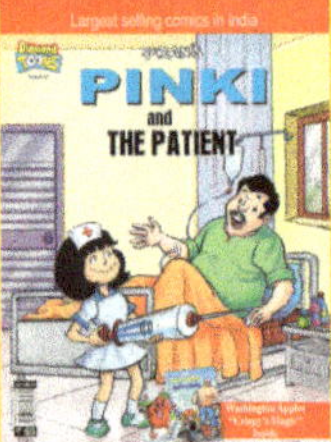

AVAILABLE IN DIGEST

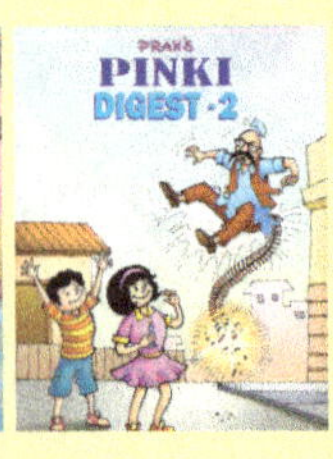

X-30 Okhla Industrial Area, Phase-II, New Delhi-110020
Ph: 011-40712200 e-mail: sales@dpb.in website: www.diamondbook.in

www.ingramcontent.com/pod-product-compliance
Lightning Source LLC
LaVergne TN
LVHW020611200726
843509LV00001B/47